Families

Aunts

Revised
and
Updated

by Lola M. Schaefer

Consulting Editor: Gail Saunders-Smith, PhD

Mankato, Minnesota

Pebble Books are published by Capstone Press,
151 Good Counsel Drive, P.O. Box 669, Mankato, Minnesota 56002.
www.capstonepress.com

1 2 3 4 5 6 13 12 11 10 09 08

Library of Congress Cataloging-in-Publication Data
Schaefer, Lola M., 1950–
    Aunts/by Lola M. Schaefer. — Rev. and updated.
    p. cm. — (Pebble books. Families)
    Includes bibliographical references and index.
    Summary: "Simple text and photographs present aunts and how they interact with
their families" — Provided by publisher.
    ISBN-13: 978-1-4296-1220-3 (hardcover)
    ISBN-10: 1-4296-1220-7 (hardcover)
    ISBN-13: 978-1-4296-1749-9 (softcover)
    ISBN-10: 1-4296-1749-7 (softcover)
    1. Aunts — Juvenile literature. 2. Nieces — Juvenile literature. 3. Nephews —
Juvenile literature. I. Title. II. Series.
HQ759.94.S33 2008
306.87 — dc22   2007027025

Note to Parents and Teachers

The Families set supports national social studies standards related
to identifying family members and their roles in the family. This
book describes and illustrates aunts. The images support early
readers in understanding the text. The repetition of words and
phrases helps early readers learn new words. This book also
introduces early readers to subject-specific vocabulary words, which
are defined in the glossary section. Early readers may need some
assistance to read some words and to use the Table of Contents,
Glossary, Read More, Internet Sites, and Index sections of the book.

Table of Contents

Aunts

Aunts are sisters
of mothers and fathers.

sisters

mother

aunt

nieces

Aunts live nearby
or far away.

Nieces and Nephews

Aunts have nieces
and nephews.

What Aunts Do

Aunt Laura calls
every Sunday.

Aunt Julia comes
to birthday parties.

Aunt Mandy plays cards.

Aunt Ida goes camping.

Aunt Sammy cuddles.

Aunts love.

Glossary

cuddle — to hold someone closely and lovingly in your arms

father — a male parent; your aunt is your father's sister.

mother — a female parent; your aunt is your mother's sister.

nephew — the son of a brother or sister

niece — the daughter of a brother or sister

sister — a girl or a woman who has the same parents as another person

Read More

Coyle, Carmela LaVigna. *Thank You, Aunt Tallulah!* Flagstaff, Ariz.: Rising Moon, 2006.

West, Colin. *Uncle Pat and Auntie Pat.* Read-It! Chapter Books. Minneapolis: Picture Window Books, 2006.

Internet Sites

FactHound offers a safe, fun way to find Internet sites related to this book. All of the sites on FactHound have been researched by our staff.

Here's how:

1. Visit *www.facthound.com*
2. Choose your grade level.
3. Type in this book ID **1429612207** for age-appropriate sites. You may also browse subjects by clicking on letters, or by clicking on pictures and words.
4. Click on the **Fetch It** button.

FactHound will fetch the best sites for you!

Index

Aunt Ida, 17
Aunt Julia, 13
Aunt Laura, 11
Aunt Mandy, 15
Aunt Sammy, 19
birthday parties, 13
camping, 17

fathers, 5
mothers, 5
nephews, 9
nieces, 9
playing, 15
sisters, 5
telephone calls, 11

Word Count: 42
Grade 1
Early-Intervention Level: 10

Editorial Credits
Sarah L. Schuette, revised edition editor; Kim Brown, revised edition designer

Photo Credits
Capstone Press/Karon Dubke, all